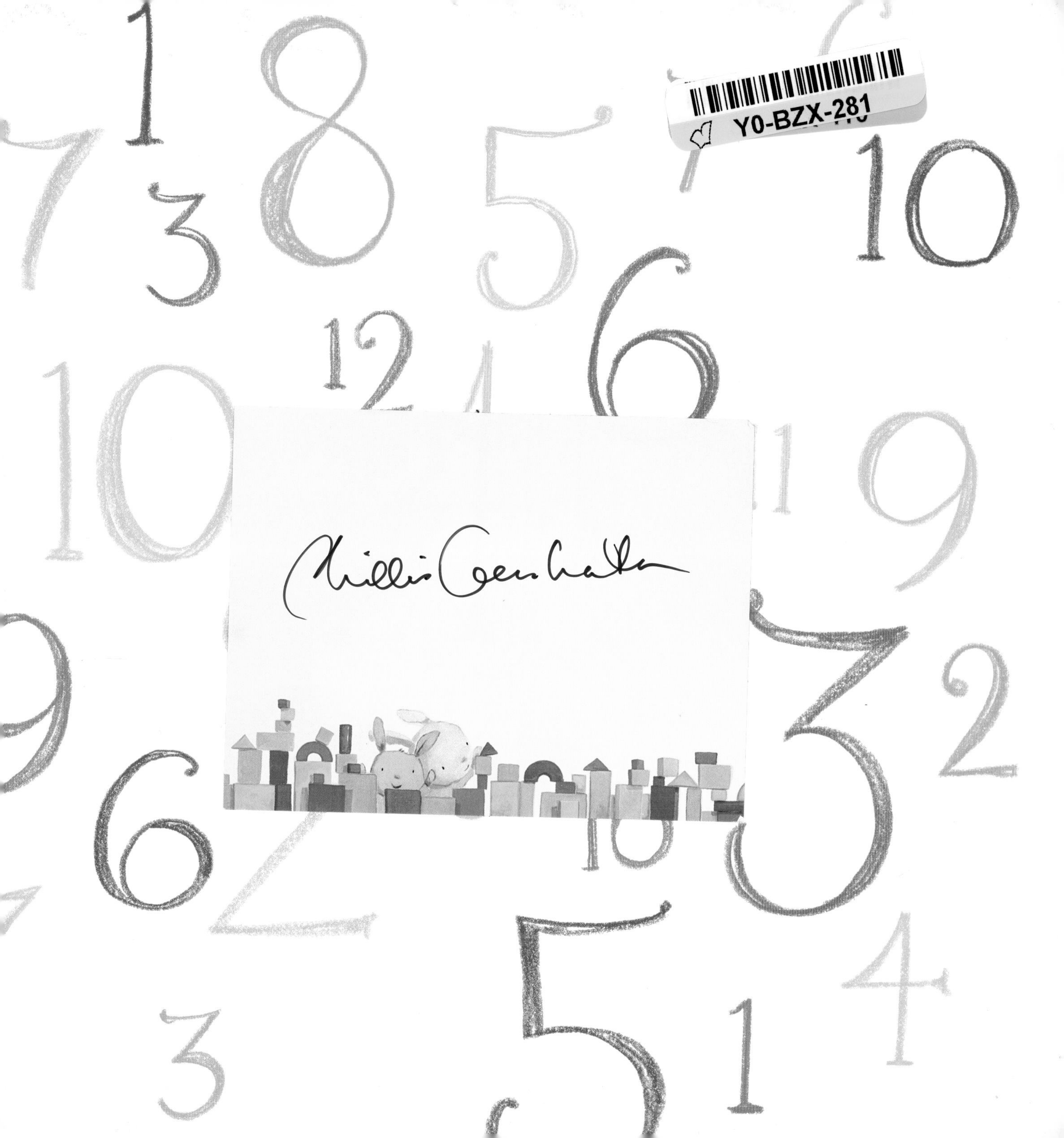

STERLING CHILDREN'S BOOKS
New York

An Imprint of Sterling Publishing
387 Park Avenue South
New York, NY 10016

ISBN 978-1-4027-7862-9

Distributed in Canada by Sterling Publishing
c/o Canadian Manda Group, 165 Dufferin Street
Toronto, Ontario, Canada M6K 3H6
Distributed in the United Kingdom by GMC Distribution Services
Castle Place, 166 High Street, Lewes, East Sussex, England BN7 1XU
Distributed in Australia by Capricorn Link (Australia) Pty. Ltd.
P.O. Box 704, Windsor, NSW 2756, Australia

For information about custom editions, special sales, and premium and corporate purchases,
please contact Sterling Special Sales at 800-805-5489 or specialsales@sterlingpublishing.com.

Printed in China
Lot #:
4 6 8 10 9 7 5
06/12

www.sterlingpublishing.com/kids

Designed by Katrina Damkoehler.

TIME
for a
HUG

Phillis Gershator and Mim Green

illustrated by David Walker

STERLING CHILDREN'S BOOKS
New York

Wake up! Wake up!
The day is new.
The clock says eight.
What shall we do?

Wash our faces,
comb our hair,

choose the clothes
we like to wear.

Eat from a bowl,
drink from a mug—

What time is it?

Time for a hug!

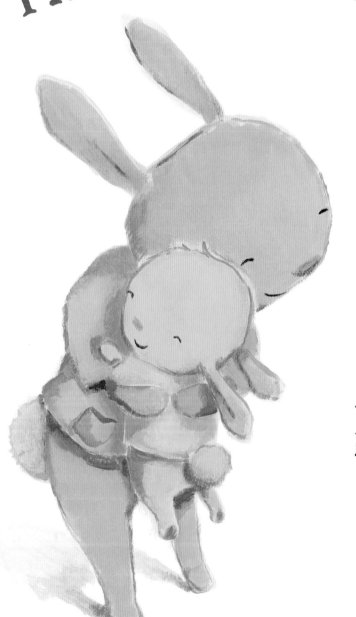

A hug feels good.
Let's hug again.

We'll hug at nine.

We'll hug at ten.

Eleven, twelve,
the raindrops fly.

What shall we do?
Let's bake a pie!

Let's make puppets
out of socks,

build a city
out of blocks,

read a book,
snuggle on the rug—

What time is it?

Time for a hug!

You'll hug me
and I'll hug you.

We'll hug until
the sun shines through.

The clock says one.
The sky is blue!

Two o'clock, three o'clock.
What shall we do?

Bounce a ball,

ride a bike,

climb a tree,

go on a hike.

Smell a flower,

chase a bug—

What time is it?

Time for a hug!

Four, five, six.
It's getting late.
Soon it will be
seven, eight.

The moon comes out.
The stars shine, too.
The clock says eight.
What shall we do?

Bathe, brush, floss,
say goodnight,

hop off to bed,
turn out the light.

Pull up the covers
warm and snug—

What time is it?

Time for a hug!

A big bear hug
and a little hug, too.

Every hug says
I LOVE YOU!

9 2 6 5 11

10 3 4

6 3

11

5 6

8 10

2 7 3

9 4 10

11 3 8 6